'After a quick peep round to make sure that nobody was watching, Ursula opened the door of the jeep and climbed in.

She quickly discovered that there was nowhere for her to hide. "Bother!" she said. "I'm much too big to squeeze under the seats. Now what do I do?"

And then Ursula had an idea . . .'

Ursula is a girl with a very special magic secret. She can turn herself into a real, live little bear! And when she discovers, on holiday in Canada, that all the bears in the National Park are kept well away from everybody, she knows that she must use her magic – and go exploring.

URSULA EXPLORING is the fourth title in a series about Ursula Bear.

D0994724

Also available by Sheila Lavelle, and published by Young Corgi Books:

URSULA CAMPING
URSULA SAILING
URSULA CLIMBING

URSULA EXPLORING is one of a series of books specially selected for beginner readers, BY MYSELF books. Other BY MYSELF books available from Young Corgi Books include:

T.R. BEAR series by Terrance Dicks
THE BIG OLD HORSE by Evelyn Davies
ALIX AND THE TIGERS by
    Alexander McCall Smith
DRAGON AIR by Ann Ruffell
A GIFT OF SQUARES by Edel Wignell

URSULA EXPLORING

URSULA EXPLORING

Sheila Lavelle

Illustrated by Thelma Lambert

YOUNG CORGI BOOKS

MORAY DISTRICT COUNCIL

DEPARTMENT OF

LEISURE AND LIBRARIES

JC

502917

URSULA EXPLORING

A YOUNG CORGI BOOK 0 552 525421

Originally published in Great Britain by
Hamish Hamilton Children's Books Ltd.

PRINTING HISTORY

Hamish Hamilton edition published 1980
Young Corgi edition published 1989

Copyright © 1980 by Sheila Lavelle
Illustrations copyright © 1980, 1989 by Thelma Lambert

Conditions of sale
1. This book is sold subject to the condition that it shall not, by
way of trade *or otherwise*, be lent, re-sold, hired out or otherwise
circulated in any form of binding or cover other than that in
which it is published *and without a similar condition including
this condition being imposed on the subsequent purchaser.*
2. This book is sold subject to the Standard Conditions of Sale
of Net Books and may not be re-sold in the UK below the net
price fixed by the publishers for the book.

This book is set in 14/18 pt Century Textbook
by Colset Private Limited, Singapore.

Young Corgi Books are published by Transworld Publishers
Ltd., 61–63 Uxbridge Road, Ealing, London W5 5SA, in
Australia by Transworld Publishers (Australia) Pty. Ltd., 15–23
Helles Avenue, Moorebank, NSW 2170, and in New Zealand by
Transworld Publishers (N.Z.) Ltd., Cnr. Moselle and Waipareira
Avenues, Henderson, Auckland.

Made and printed in Great Britain by
The Guernsey Press Co. Ltd, Guernsey
Channel Islands

Ursula Exploring

Chapter One

One of the nicest things about eating
your dinner in an aeroplane, Ursula
thought, was the special plastic tray
it was served on, with all its separate
little spaces. One for your meat
course, one for your pudding, one for
your cheese and biscuits, and even

one for your coffee cup.

It was steak and kidney pie and apple crumble, one of Ursula's favourite meals, but she was too excited to feel very hungry. She was so excited she could hardly sit still,

for here she was, at last, on her way to Canada, the land of the bears.

Ursula was very fond of bears. In fact, Ursula liked bears so much that she hardly ever thought about anything else. And if she wasn't thinking

about bears she would be talking about bears, or drawing pictures of bears, or reading books about bears, or singing songs about bears, or sticking photos of bears in her bear scrapbook.

Ursula looked out of the window at the shining silver sea far below, and the clouds piled up like cream on a trifle.

'Are you all right, Ursula?' said Aunt Prudence from the next seat.

'Oh yes,' said Ursula. 'It's lovely. But are you sure they've got bears in Canada?'

Aunt Prudence smiled.

'Of course they've got bears,' she said. 'They've got great big National Parks, with forests and lakes and things. The bears roam around wild, living in caves and catching fish from the streams. I've seen them on the telly.'

Aunt Prudence knew that Ursula loved bears better than anything else in the world. But what she didn't know was that Ursula had a secret. A very special magic secret.

Ursula knew how to turn herself into a real live bear whenever she liked. A small cuddly brown bear, with a velvet coat and shiny black eyes. And all because of a simple magic spell.

Ursula had found the spell in a book in the library. You could even try it yourself some time. All you need is a currant bun, filled with a mixture of honey and porridge oats. All the things that bears like best. And while you eat it you must say the magic words.

'I'M A BEAR, I'M A BEAR, I'M A BEAR,

'I'M A BEAR, I'M A BEAR, I'M A BEAR.'

And it really works. Well, it did for Ursula anyway.

Ursula could hardly wait for the plane to land, but at long last it touched down on the runway at Edmonton Airport. Uncle Angus and

Aunt Grace were waiting to meet them, and there was a lot of hugging and kissing and laughing and crying.

Ursula watched carefully as Uncle Angus put her new brown suitcase into the boot of his car. She had to keep an eye on it because tucked away at the bottom was a small parcel wrapped in greaseproof paper. A currant bun, filled with porridge oats and honey. You never knew when it might be useful.

Chapter Two

Ursula took her little parcel with her to all the places they visited in Canada. And it was safely hidden in the back pocket of her jeans when Uncle Angus drove them all to Rocky Rapids National Park the very next Sunday. He stopped the car under some trees and Ursula quickly scrambled out to look for bears.

Uncle Angus pushed his hat back from his red face.

'Well, what do you think of Rocky Rapids, Ursula?' he said.

Ursula looked, and her heart almost sank into her plimsolls. Rocky Rapids was worse than Brighton Beach. There were tents and trailers and cars

and coaches and caravans and hot dog stalls and ice-cream vans and transistor radios. There were hundreds of people everywhere, and there wasn't a single bear in sight.

The three grown-ups made themselves comfortable on some deck-chairs in the shade and got ready for a pleasant nap. Ursula kicked grumpily at a pebble with her toe and scowled.

'You said there'd be bears,' she said to Aunt Prudence crossly.

'Oh, there's bears all right,' said Uncle Angus. 'That forest's full of them. They never come near the picnic places, though. The park rangers make sure of that. Bears can be real nasty sometimes.' And he lay back in his chair and put his hanky over his face.

'Why don't you go off and explore, Ursula dear,' said Aunt Prudence. 'You might find some nice little friends to play with.'

Ursula scowled harder than ever. She didn't want any nice little friends

to play with. What she wanted was to see some bears.

'I knew we should have gone to Russia,' she muttered. She patted the pocket of her jeans to make sure her small parcel was still there, then she set off across the field towards the forest. If there were bears in there she would find them herself.

Chapter Three

Ursula walked on, past the noisy shooting range and the hot dog stand, until she came to a small wooden house. It was the park ranger's log cabin, and a notice on the door suddenly caught Ursula's eye.

Safari Trips 5 Dollars

Follow the Nature Trail into the forest in our Safari Jeep. See the famous waterfall at Rocky Rapids and the wild black bears of Grizzly Valley

Next trip two o'clock.

Parked beside the cabin was a battered old army jeep, with the words SAFARI BUS painted on its side.

Ursula held her breath and stared. Five dollars was a lot of money, and she didn't have anything like that amount. She looked over her shoulder at where she had left the grown-ups, but they all seemed to be fast asleep. They wouldn't be at all pleased if she woke them up, Ursula thought.

She gazed at the notice once more. 'Wild black bears of Grizzly Valley!' she breathed. 'I've just got to see them.'

All at once she made up her mind. After a quick peep round to make sure that nobody was watching, Ursula opened the door of the jeep and climbed in.

She quickly discovered that there was nowhere for her to hide. 'Bother!' she said. 'I'm much too big to squeeze under the seats. Now what do I do?'

And then Ursula had an idea, for there was just enough room under the seat to hide a very small brown *bear*.

There was only one thing to do, and Ursula did it.

Without wasting any more time Ursula pulled the paper bag from her pocket and unwrapped the squashed and sticky currant bun. She gobbled it down so fast she almost choked,

and it was a bit difficult saying the magic words with her mouth so full. At last she managed to swallow the last bite, so she closed her eyes, crossed her fingers and waited.

A few minutes later, Ursula heard voices outside the jeep. The doors

opened and a family of Americans got in, a mother and father and two small boys. The boys were squabbling noisily about who should have the best seat, but finally they all settled down. Then the park ranger climbed into the driving seat, without noticing a small brown furry bundle curled up beneath it. The spell had worked just in time, and Ursula had once more turned into Ursula Bear.

Chapter Four

Ursula kept herself as small as possible and hardly dared to breathe as the jeep began to bump its way over the rough grass towards the forest.

It was a very bumpy ride. Ursula's teeth were almost rattled out of her head as the jeep jolted along the stony trail. She could hear the children exclaiming over the wonderful view, and soon she began to feel very fed up indeed.

'This isn't much fun,' she growled to herself crossly. 'All I've got a wonderful view of is the driver's boots.'

Suddenly the jeep lurched to a stop and the ranger got out.

'We'll take a little walk here,' he said. 'You can see Rocky Falls from just around this bend.' Everybody climbed out and Ursula could hear their voices fading into the distance.

When the jeep was empty, Ursula crawled stiffly out from under the seat. She stretched her cramped legs and wiped the dust from her nose with her paws. Then she scrambled up on to the driver's seat to peep out of the open window.

Ursula almost jumped out of her furry skin. A small boy with curly hair and a freckled face was peering in at

her from outside, and he looked just as astonished to see Ursula as she was to see him.

'Hey, Pa!' shouted the boy. 'Come quick! There's a bear in the jeep!'

Ursula heard the sound of running feet. The park ranger came dashing out from the trees, pulling his gun from its holster.

The boy pointed at Ursula. 'Look!' he shouted excitedly. 'It's a bear. I came back to get my Fruity Bar and there it was.'

The ranger grabbed the boy and pushed him away from the jeep. 'Stay out of the way, kid,' he said. 'I'll take care of this.'

Ursula was too frightened to move. She was still standing on the seat

with her two front paws on the
steering wheel. The ranger stared in
at her and Ursula stared back.
Suddenly the ranger laughed.

'It's only a cub,' he called. 'Come
on, it won't hurt you.'

The rest of the family came
nervously back to the jeep, the
mother clinging tightly to her
husband's arm. They all gazed at
Ursula with wide eyes.

'It's cute,' said the boy. 'Can we take it home, Pa?'

The ranger opened the door and lifted Ursula to the ground. 'His own Ma and Pa will probably be looking for him,' he said. 'I think we'd best be on our way before they turn up.'

He gave Ursula a little push towards the forest. 'Off you go, little one,' he said. They all climbed back into the jeep and drove away, with the boys hanging out of the windows for a last glimpse of the little bear.

Ursula watched them disappear down the trail. She suddenly felt very small and lonely. She sat down under a tree and listened to the birds singing and the sound of running water somewhere nearby.

'Well, I might as well have a look at Rocky Falls while I'm here,' she said to herself.

Chapter Five

Ursula followed the winding track through the trees. The sound of water grew louder and louder until at last she came to a rocky ledge. She leaned over the edge and looked down.

Below her she could see a waterfall, tumbling and splashing over the rocks and making clouds of white spray. At the bottom of the waterfall was a swirling pool, surrounded by large flat rocks. The sun shone down through the leaves and made a tiny rainbow in the spray, and Ursula thought it was the loveliest place she had ever seen.

But it wasn't the waterfall or the pool or even the rainbow that made Ursula's black eyes gleam and her knees wobble with excitement. For playing by the water and among the rocks was a whole family of real live bears.

Ursula stared and stared. There were five of them altogether. The biggest of them was standing in the pool swiping at something in the

water with a huge black paw. Three small cubs were romping at the edge, while another large bear basked in the sun and kept an eye on them from a nearby rock. Ursula watched as the biggest bear knocked a glittering silver fish out of the water on to the bank. The three cubs pounced on it with squeals of delight and began to growl over their dinner.

Ursula tried very hard not to make any sound, but she was so thrilled that she couldn't help making an excited sort of squeak. And at once the whole family of bears turned round and stared up at her.

The bears gazed up at Ursula for what seemed like a very long time. At

last the biggest bear began to wave his paws at her in a friendly manner, and one of the cubs picked up a piece of the fish and held it up towards her.

Ursula gulped. 'Oh!' she said. 'I think they like me. I think they're inviting me to dinner.' And she began to pick her way carefully down the rocky slope towards the waiting bears.

Ursula was half expecting to be gobbled up at once, but she needn't have worried. The bears were as friendly as could be. And so Ursula spent the whole of the afternoon in the leafy hollow by the pool. She romped and tumbled and wrestled with the three cuddly young cubs. She swam and paddled in the water

and dried her fur on the rocks in the sun. She climbed trees looking for wild bees' honey and ate nuts and wild berries. She even tried a bit of the father bear's raw fish and was

surprised at how good it tasted. It was the happiest afternoon of her life, and Ursula wished it could go on for ever.

But all too soon the sun began to sink in the sky and Ursula knew it was time for her to leave her new friends. The bears seemed sorry to see her go, and they stood together in a little group to watch her as she climbed back up the cliff towards the trail. She paused at the top to wave goodbye, and after a last look at the cubs she sadly turned away and set off on the long walk back to her family.

Chapter Six

It was a very dusty and weary little
bear that limped out of the forest
some time later. At last she was back
in the meadow, but now Ursula had to
turn herself into a girl again before
she could return to her uncle and
aunts. Beefburgers and chips were

the only things that would work the second part of the spell, but how was she to get them in a place like this?

Ursula looked across the field at the hot dog stall. 'Hamburgers!' she growled softly. 'I bet they'd do the trick.'

But Ursula had quite forgotten what might happen when a small brown bear suddenly appears in a field full of people, and before she

could reach the hot dog stall she found she was causing a panic. People started running about shouting, 'Look out! It's a bear!' and 'Get the ranger before it bites somebody!'

The park ranger arrived almost at once, and he was very surprised to see Ursula. He looked at her closely and scratched his head.

'Not you again, is it?' he said. 'This is no place for little bears. I'd better get the jeep and take you back to the forest.' And he picked Ursula up and began to carry her towards his cabin.

Ursula struggled and whimpered in the ranger's arms. She patted her stomach and made growling noises, and pointed at her mouth with her paw. The ranger laughed.

'You must be hungry after that

long walk,' he said. 'All right, come on. I'll buy you a bun.'

But Ursula shook her head firmly when the ranger offered a large sticky bun, and pointed her paw hopefully at the hamburgers sizzling away in a frying pan.

'You're a funny sort of bear,' said the ranger. 'Bears are supposed to like buns.' But Ursula kept on pointing until at last the ranger gave in.

'One large hamburger for the bear,' he said to the astonished attendant, and Ursula was very pleased to see that it was served with chips, and lots of tomato ketchup. Now she had everything she needed for the magic spell.

'You can eat your dinner in peace

while I get the jeep,' the ranger told Ursula kindly. He unlocked the cabin door and left her sitting on the table with the carton of food.

'RAEB A M'I, RAEB A M'I, RAEB A M'I,

'RAEB A M'I, RAEB A M'I, RAEB A M'I.'

Ursula growled the magic words backwards through a mouthful of hot chips. 'I hope hamburgers work the same as beefburgers.'

As soon as she had eaten the last scrap, Ursula curled herself into a ball and shut her eyes tight.

The park ranger never saw that small brown bear again. When he came back a little while later he found the window swinging open and the

cabin empty. Ursula had changed back into herself again, climbed out of the window, and slipped quickly away.

Ursula was panting for breath and quite worn out when she reached the deckchairs under the trees where she had left the grown-ups. She flopped down on the grass by their feet.

'Oh, there you are,' said Aunt Prudence. 'We were getting quite anxious about you. Where on earth have you been all day?'

'I did just what you told me,' said Ursula. 'I went exploring. And I found some nice little friends to play with.'

'Well, I'm afraid there's not much picnic left,' said Aunt Prudence. 'And the poor child must be starving.'

'Never mind,' said Uncle Angus. 'I know just what she'd like.' He got up from his chair and pulled Ursula to her feet.

'Come on, Ursula,' he said. 'I'll buy

you a great big juicy hamburger for
your tea.'

URSULA CAMPING

BY Sheila Lavelle
ILLUSTRATED BY Thelma Lambert

Ursula is an ordinary girl – with one special dif-
ference. If she eats a currant bun, stuffed with a
mixture of porridge oats and honey, and recites
a magic spell, she can turn herself into a real,
live, little bear!

When she runs up against trouble from her two
cousins, Ian and Jamie, while on a camping holiday in the New Forest, Ursula finds that being
able to change herself into a bear can be very
useful indeed . . .

0 552 524476

URSULA SAILING

BY SHEILA LAVELLE
ILLUSTRATED BY THELMA LAMBERT

Ursula is an ordinary girl – with one very special secret. She can turn herself into a real, live, little bear! Sometimes this can be very useful, especially when there is a tall and difficult tree to climb. But in this new adventure for Ursula, she soon discovers that rivers and boats mean trouble for bears . . .

0 552 524484

URSULA CLIMBING

BY SHEILA LAVELLE
ILLUSTRATED BY THELMA LAMBERT

Ursula is an ordinary girl but she has an unusual secret. She can turn herself into a real, live, little bear!

On a visit to Wales, Ursula has a wonderful time – until a huge buzzard swoops down and seizes her favourite teddy, Fredbear. As Fredbear is carried high up a cliff to the buzzard's nest, Ursula knows that she needs to use her special magic to try and save him . . .

THE AMAZING PET

BY MARJORIE NEWMAN
ILLUSTRATED BY ELAINE MACGREGOR
TURNEY

Everyone in Robert's family is amazingly good at something – except Robert. And he's fed up with being ordinary. But then he has a thought. He will have a pet. Nothing ordinary like a cat or dog. No, Robert is determined to have an *amazing* pet – and what could be more amazing than a giraffe? He's never heard of anyone having a giraffe for a pet before!

But what will Mum and Dad say when Robert's giraffe, George, comes home? Will they like him as much as he does? Perhaps he should keep it all a secret until everything is ready . . .

0 552 52469 7

ALIX AND THE TIGERS

BY ALEXANDER MCCALL SMITH
ILLUSTRATED BY JON MILLER

The two elderly tigers, Mah-Var and Mah-Baja, are Alix's favourite animals at the zoo. She's not even frightened when they escape. Surely they are too old and gentle to hurt anyone . . .

But there's a cruel hunter on their trail – with orders to shoot them! Alix knows she must act fast if she is to save the tigers . . .

A hilarious story from the author of *The Perfect Hamburger* and *Mike's Magic Seeds*.

0 552 52477 8

YOUNG CORGI

If you would like to receive a Newsletter about our new Children's books, just fill in the coupon below with your name and address (or copy it onto a separate piece of paper if you don't want to spoil your book) and send it to:

The Children's Books Editor
Young Corgi Books
61–63 Uxbridge Road,
Ealing
London W5 5SA

Please send me a Children's Newsletter:

Name . . . .

Address . . . .

. . . .

. . . .

All Children's Books are available at your bookshop or newsagent, or can be ordered from the following address:
Corgi/Bantam Books,
Cash Sales Department,
P.O. Box 11, Falmouth, Cornwall TR10 9EN

Please send a cheque or postal order (no currency) and allow 60p for postage and packing for the first book plus 25p for the second book and 15p for each additional book ordered up to a maximum charge of £1.90 in UK.

B.F.P.O. customers please allow 60p for the first book, 25p for the second book plus 15p per copy for the next 7 books, thereafter 9p per book.

Overseas customers, including Eire, please allow £1.25 for postage and packing for the first book, 75p for the second book, and 28p for each subsequent title ordered.